Little Red Rid

Once upon a ti.
known to all as Little Red Riding Hood.
One day, her mother gave her a
basket of cakes and asked her
daughter to take the basket to
her grandmother who lived
across the wood.

As the little girl walked through the forest, a wolf stepped out from the trees and asked Little Red Riding Hood where she was going. "I am taking these cakes to Grandma, sir," replied the girl. "Why, how nice of you, child," said the wolf. "Why don't you pick some beautiful spring flowers for her as well?"

Little Red Riding Hood followed the wolf's suggestion and wandered off the path to gather flowers. Meanwhile, the wolf hurried off to Grandma's cottage.

The wolf rapped on the cottage door and, imitating Little Red Riding Hood's voice, asked to come inside.

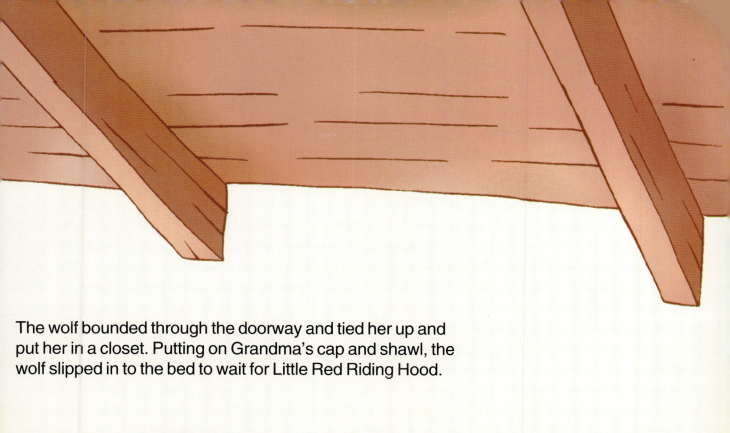

The wolf bounded through the doorway and tied her up and put her in a closet. Putting on Grandma's cap and shawl, the wolf slipped in to the bed to wait for Little Red Riding Hood.

When Little Red Riding Hood
entered the cottage, the wolf,
this time imitating Grandma's voice,
asked her to come closer. Drawing
nearer, the girl said, "Grandma, what big ears
you have!" "The better to hear you with, dearie,
"answered the wolf.

"And what big eyes you have, Grandma."
"All the better to see you, my sweet."
"Oh, what a long nose you have!"
"The better to smell you with, my lamb."
"Goodness, what a big mouth you have, Grandma."
"The better to eat you with!"
roared the wolf.

The wolf sprang from the bed after Little Red Riding Hood.

A hunter who happened to be passing by heard the
wolf howling and the girl's frightened screams.
He stopped to investigate.

Seeing the hunter, the wolf ran away and escaped.

Little Red Riding Hood told the hunter that her Grandmother was missing. They searched the house and found her in the closet safe and unharmed. They all lived happily ever after.